CULTURE ISLAND
How Captain Tall Tale Became Tall
PART: 2

written by:
Todd McClain

edited by:
Christina Gray

illustrated by:
Cecilia Coto

CAPTAIN TALL TALE BOOK SERIES

Original Title:
Culture Island
How Captain Tall Tale Became Tall
Part: 2

Author: Todd McClain
1° edition June 2018

Editor: Christina Gray
www.thescriptconsultant.com

Illustrations: Cecilia Coto

Copyright 2018, by Todd McClain
Captain Tall Tale, LLC

INFO@CaptainTallTale.com
ISBN: 978-1-945183-07-2
Library of Congress Control Number: 2017917392

No part of this publication may be reproduced, stored in a retrieval system, or transmitted in any form or by any means - electronic, mechanical, photocopying, recorded or otherwise without prior written permission by the Author.

All Rights Reserved

Continued Upon A Time...

Captain Tall Tale sat in the sand and thought of all the wild events that led up to this moment.

His best friend and boat had been taken by pirates. Then there were three strange beans, waking up on a beach with very long legs, and now a blue monster standing over him welcoming him to **Culture Island.**

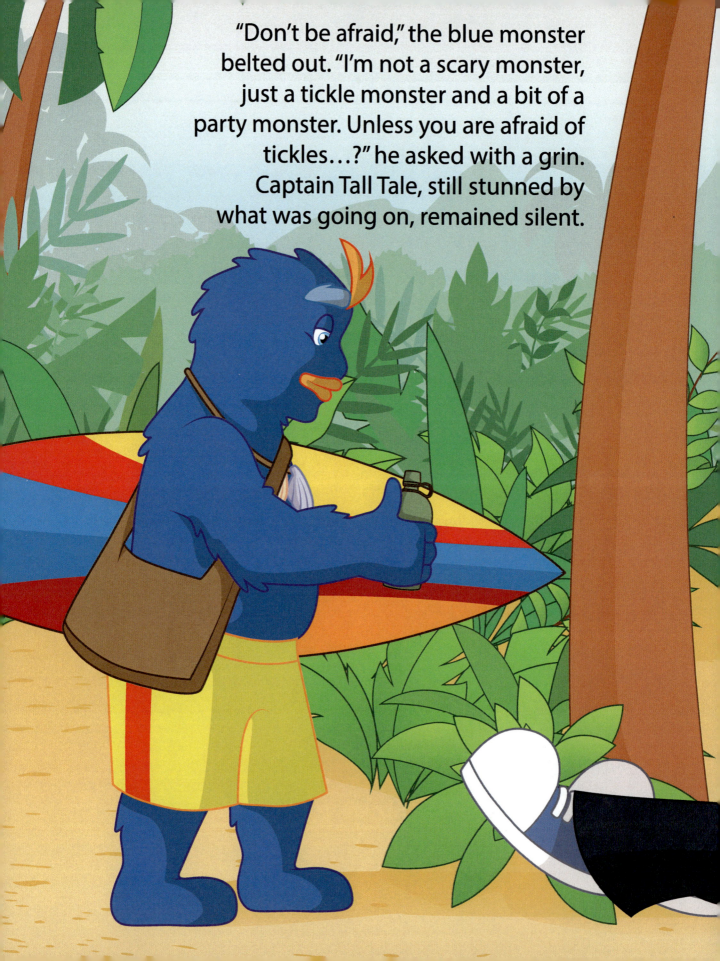

"Don't be afraid," the blue monster belted out. "I'm not a scary monster, just a tickle monster and a bit of a party monster. Unless you are afraid of tickles…?" he asked with a grin. Captain Tall Tale, still stunned by what was going on, remained silent.

Mo'Roko excitedly told Captain Tall Tale that Culture Island's inhabitants were made up of cultures from all around the world, and that everyone on the island was focused on living together in peace.

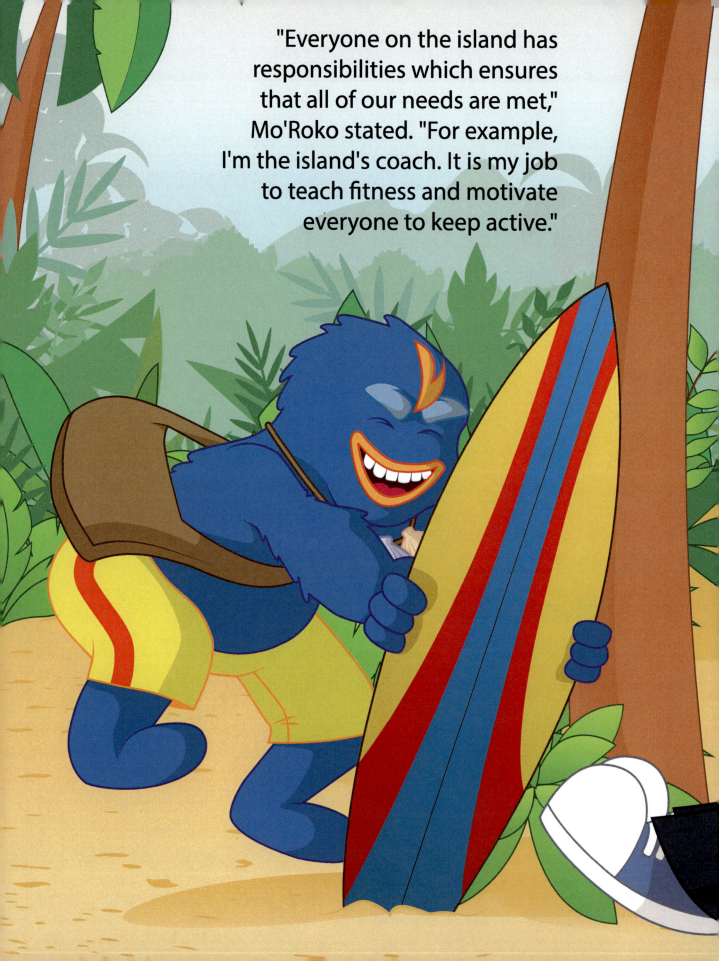

Captain Tall Tale told Mo'Roko how he ended up on the island. As he reached the end of his tale, he added how important it was that he find and save his best friend, J.R., from the pirates.

Mo'Roko was fascinated with the exciting story and told the captain that he would like to help rescue J.R.

"First things first though. We need to get you up on your legs and make sure you are able to walk around safely," Mo'Roko stated. "Then I will take you on a tour of Culture Island."

Mo'Roko helped Captain Tall Tale stand up and talked him through how to walk on his new tall legs. Mo'Roko warned him that being that tall would be different, and he would have to take his time.

Captain Tall Tale was trying his best but felt very wobbly. After losing his balance a few times, he sat in the sand, frustrated and ready to give up. "Maybe I will just crawl everywhere from now on," he said.

Mo'Roko told the captain that he understood the frustration of learning to walk with long legs. When he was young his grandfather had made him a pair of extended legs called stilts. The blue monster found two long bamboo stalks and used them to make a pair of stilts just like his grandfather had once made for him.

Mo'Roko hopped onto the stilts and walked around. He even jumped and danced, too. He told Captain Tall Tale, "You see? It is possible to walk tall!"

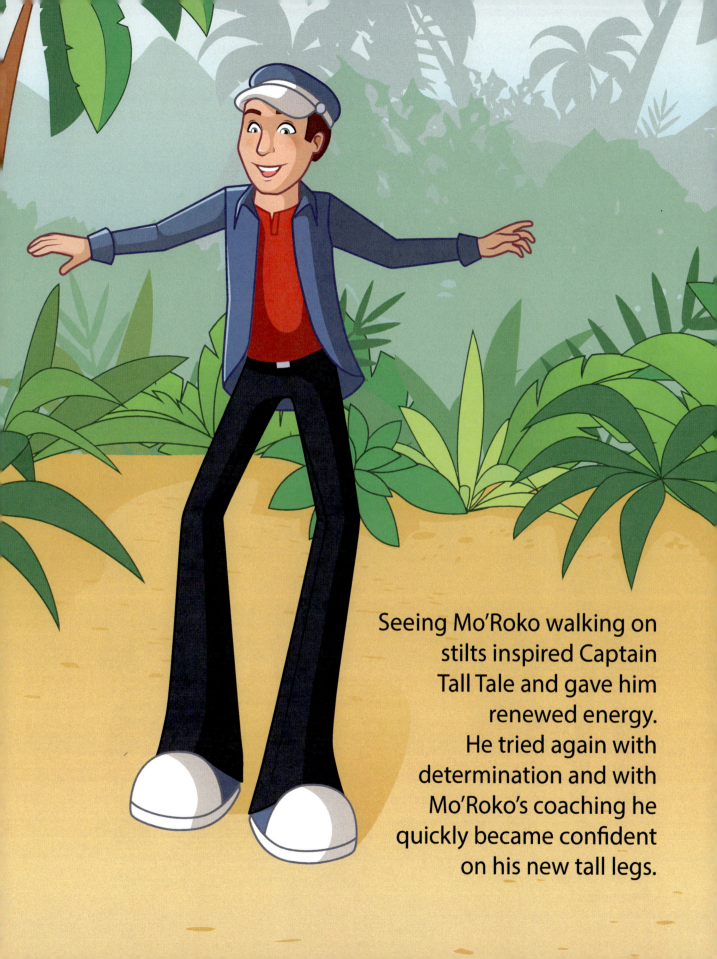

Seeing Mo'Roko walking on stilts inspired Captain Tall Tale and gave him renewed energy. He tried again with determination and with Mo'Roko's coaching he quickly became confident on his new tall legs.

Captain Tall Tale was so thrilled with the progress they made, he taught Mo'Roko the Captain Tall Tale Victory Dance to celebrate.

First cross your right fist down across your body.

Cross your left fist down across your body.

Cross your left fist up across your right shoulder.

Cross your right fist up across your left shoulder.

Pump your right fist twice in the air.

Pump your left fist twice in the air.

Launch your fist in the air as you jump and yell, "Yeah!"

And…
Dance the shake-a-lotta!
Shake your body any way you like, just as long as you feel silly.

After Captain Tall Tale finished the shake-a-lotta part of the dance, he didn't want to stop so he yelled out "Spin-a-Roo!" and spun in a circle. Then he spun back in the other direction. He then kicked up his leg as high as he could and yelled, **"WILD TIMES!"**

Mo'Roko congratulated Captain Tall Tale on his progress and assured him he was ready to tour the island. At that moment, the captain's stomach grumbled loud with hunger. They both looked at each other in surprise and snickered.

As they started their walk Captain Tall Tale asked, "What is culture?"

Mo'Roko responded, "Culture is how a group of people act when they live together as a community.

The language spoken, the types of food prepared, the styles of clothes worn, music, art, manners, customs, and of course celebrations are all types of culture."

As they entered a dense group of trees, they heard birds singing. Mo'Roko stated, "Speaking of culture, this is the **Musical Jungle** where we share music and hold most of our celebrations."

As Captain Tall Tale followed Mo'Roko out of the jungle, the blue monster pointed up at a large mountain. "The top is where Reny the Yeti lives. He is caretaker of the peaks where science and all faiths are observed and welcome."

"Flowing down the mountain is a waterfall named **Cultural Falls** which leads to my cave and home," Mo'Roko stated proudly.

Mo'Roko led Captain Tall Tale down a path that followed a small river flowing out from Cultural Falls.

They walked across a small bridge into **Hermit Crab Hideaway** where hermit crabs who came from all over the world live and work together.

Mo'Roko led the captain to a hut that looked like a seashell. The building had a French flag on top and a well-kept garden in the back.

After they knocked on the front door, a female voice from within said, "Enter!" The voice had a French accent.

As Captain Tall Tale entered, he made sure to duck but bonked his head on the low ceiling anyway.

A hermit crab with a chef's outfit met them at the door and gasped, "My, you are tall!"

Mo'Roko popped his head around from behind the captain and added, "Yes, he is tall! **Captain Tall Tale**. He washed up on the shore in a dinghy this morning. He could sure use some food, and then he can tell you his tale."

The little hermit crab introduced herself as Chef Petite. She told Captain Tall Tale that on the island it was her job to show everyone how to prepare their own food - from the garden to the kitchen. She welcomed him to have a seat as she brought him a meal.

The captain didn't see a seat that he could sit in.

Then he saw the counter which was the best proportion for him and sat there. Mo'Roko and Chef Petite were surprised, but then they understood.

After finishing his meal, Captain Tall Tale told his story. When he reached the end of the tale, Chef Petite inquired about the beans. The captain pulled out one of the two remaining beans from his pocket to show her and remarked, "There is something strange about these beans."

Just then a macaw flew in one window, grabbed the bean, and flew out another window. Mo'Roko instantly jumped up and yelled after her, "Squawk! No!" Startled, the bird dropped the bean somewhere in the garden and flew off.

All three of them ran outside into the garden and searched for the bean, but soon the sun went down and it became too dark.

They decided that it would be better to try searching in the morning when there would be better light. Mo'Roko invited Captain Tall Tale to sleep at his cave for the night. Upon leaving, they thanked Chef Petite for her hospitality, and she told them they were welcome anytime.

When they reached the cave, Captain Tall Tale instantly fell asleep in the hammock that Mo'Roko prepared for him.

The captain was suddenly woken from his sleep by Mo'Roko shaking him as he pointed to the entrance of the cave.

When they reached the entrance of the cave, Captain Tall Tale could not help but see an enormous beanstalk that had grown out of Chef Petite's garden and was reaching up to the clouds.

Amazed, the captain held up the remaining bean in his hand, looked at Mo'Roko and said, "We really need to find J.R. so that we can know the story behind these beans!"

THE END

Join Captain Tall Tale on his next adventure as he tries to save his best friend and learn the secret of the magic beans in:

MAGIC BEANS

How Captain Tall Tale Became Tall
PART: 3

Cecilia Coto illustrator:

Cecilia Coto is a graphic designer and an illustrator with a keen ability to make designs that range from fun and playful to serious and classic. She specializes and loves creating striking character logos, cartoon logos, identities, and traditional or classic logos.

2015 has been an excellent doorway, opportunity to develop her skills as an illustrator and designer. Cecilia is a naturally creative person and passionate about illustration because it is a way to show all her creativity in a project.

Originally from and still residing in a little country in Central America not many people know of called El Salvador. She spends her time working with new clients to create art, and enjoying her large and close family. Her passions are traveling, watching movies and eating sushi.

All of Cecilia's clients have given high praises for her work that is featured in many countries like United States, Switzerland, Canada, England, and Singapore. She is humbled and very glad that she can make so many people happy with her art and creations.

For more information about Cecilia Coto go to:
www.87graphics.com

For more information about Captain Tall Tale go to:
www.CaptainTallTale.com

Made in the USA
Columbia, SC
06 May 2022